TORNADO

Sharon Jennings

orca soundings

ORCA BOOK PUBLISHERS

Published in Canada and the United States in 2021 by Orca Book Publishers.
orcabook.com

Library and Archives Canada Cataloguing in Publication
Title: Tornado / Sharon Jennings.
Names: Jennings, Sharon, 1954– author.
Series: Orca soundings.
Description: Series statement: Orca soundings
Identifiers: Canadiana (print) 20200274317 | Canadiana (ebook) 20200274325 |
ISBN 9781459827264 (softcover) | ISBN 9781459827271 (PDF) |
ISBN 9781459827288 (EPUB)
Classification: LCC PS8569.E563 T67 2021 | DDC jc813/.54—dc23

Library of Congress Control Number: 2020939281

Summary: In this high-interest accessible novel for teen readers,
sixteen-year-old Cam must find his way home to save his little
brother when a tornado hits.

Orca Book Publishers is committed to reducing the consumption
of nonrenewable resources in the making of our books. We make
every effort to use materials that support a sustainable future.

Orca Book Publishers gratefully acknowledges the support for its
publishing programs provided by the following agencies: the Government
of Canada, the Canada Council for the Arts and the Province of British
Columbia through the BC Arts Council and the Book Publishing Tax Credit.

Edited by Tanya Trafford
Design by Ella Collier
Cover photography by Shutterstock.com/lafoto (front) and
Shutterstock.com/Krasovski Dmitri (back)

Printed and bound in Canada.

24 23 22 21 • 1 2 3 4

In memory of Paul Kropp,

my mentor and friend.

Chapter One

The hot air in the portable was sickening. The only good thing about the heat was the girls. Cam stared at Ava as she unzipped her hoodie and slipped it off. She smiled at him and wiggled her bare shoulders. Her pink tank top stretched tight.

Cam grinned and looked down at the test booklet on his desk. *Focus, idiot.*

"You know the rules," the teacher said. "No talking. No bathroom breaks. No nothing."

"Breathing okay?" Jake yelled.

Mr. Morgan did his usual eye roll. "Go ahead. If you can find any air in here."

Cam wondered if girls had some secret code. Like birds that turn and fly in the same direction at the same time. Because all of a sudden, every girl in the portable was playing with her hair, lifting it off her neck, shaking her head. Cam smelled the fruity, flowery shampoos and conditioners and deodorants. He moaned. There was no way he was going to get through this exam. Even if he *had* studied for it. His parents would kill him if he failed one more test.

"Everyone okay with me turning off the lights?" Mr. Morgan asked. "I think it's bright enough."

But before he could get to the switch, the lights went out. "That's weird," he said. He fumbled with the intercom. "Not working either. Adam, can you please go to the office and find out what's happening?"

"Can we talk now?" asked Ava.

"Turn your exams over. Pens down." Mr. Morgan glanced around the room.

A few minutes later someone from the office walked into the classroom with Adam. "Power's out," she said. "There's a storm over in Midland, and the generator is down. We're closing the school." She smiled at the class. "Happy long weekend, everybody!"

Mr. Morgan had to shout over the cheering. "We will do the exam first thing Monday morning. Don't forget to hand in your booklets before you leave."

Cam dropped his test on the pile and leaped from the door of the portable to the ground.

Adam grabbed him by his shirt. "I've got my mom's car. Do you want to come for burgers with us?" He had his other arm around Chrissy.

"I'm in!" Cam had three free hours until he had to get his brother, Peter, from the school bus. His parents would never know he'd taken off.

Ava leaned in close. "I'm coming too," she whispered in his ear.

"Sweet!" Cam said. "Won't your mom kill you, though, hanging out with me?"

"Who's going to tell her?" Chrissy asked with a grin.

They raced to the parking lot. The roof was down on the BMW, and Cam swung himself into the back seat.

Ava squeezed in beside him and did up her seat belt. She snuggled in close to Cam and slid one leg over his.

They hit the road and soon reached the highway. Adam shouted over his shoulder. "We're going to Harry's Burger Joint in Halton!"

Cam gave him a thumbs-up.

Adam headed south, driving fast and passing other cars. Cam leaned back, his head on the leather. *Someday I'm going to have a BMW. Two of them, like Adam's dad. One for me, one for my girlfriend.*

He looked at Ava. A piece of her long hair flew in his face, catching on his mouth. He pretended to eat it, pulling her face to his. She laughed before kissing him.

When they broke apart, Cam stared up at the blue sky. Not a cloud anywhere. *Like my life.* And it was true. A hot day in June. A freak Friday off school. Perfect car. Perfect girlfriend. Perfect summer job lined up at the marina. Cam smiled. He forgot about his dad yelling at him, calling him a loser. About his mom drinking, crying, all the time. Avoiding him. He was sixteen. Not much longer before he was out of the house. And he would never have to listen to them again.

About half an hour later, they pulled off the highway at Harry's Burger Joint. It was busy. Lots of people heading up north for the weekend, Cam figured. He noticed several cars towing boats. Some of them had huge inboards. *That's another thing I want.* Cam pictured himself and Ava on a yacht in the Caribbean. She was in a bikini, her hair blowing in the wind.

"Why are you smiling?" Ava asked.

"Thinking about you."

Ava laughed. "With or without clothes?"

He grabbed her and pulled her in for another kiss. "You can read minds?"

"Just yours, Cam." She held his chin and looked into his eyes. "You're my man," she whispered.

They ordered burgers with fries and drinks and then grabbed a table. But the air-conditioning was cranked right up. It was freezing inside. As soon as their food was ready, they found a picnic table outside. When they sat down, Ava dumped most of her fries on Cam's plate.

"Not hungry?"

"Yes, but…I only want a couple. Just to taste."

Cam watched her peel the bun off her burger. She picked it into tiny bits and flung them onto the grass. Seagulls swooped down in seconds.

"She's on a diet," Chrissy explained. "So am I, actually. Starting after I eat this."

Cam looked at the two girls. "I don't get it. You're both...you're..." He felt himself go red.

"Hot. He's trying to say you're hot," said Adam, laughing at his friend.

Chrissy flipped her hair and giggled. "We know that," she answered. "But we need to be skinny too. We're entering the Top Model search at the mall next weekend. They scouted Martina Jag there."

"Your folks okay with that?" Cam asked Ava.

"No. That's why I'm sneaking off."

Cam nodded. Ava's parents were strict about her marks and her going to med school. That's why they didn't like Cam. *Not smart enough for their precious darling.*

"What's happening this weekend?" Adam asked. "Anyone got plans? We should keep the party going."

"My parents went to the cottage this morning. Said I could stay home *if* I studied," Chrissy offered. "They didn't say I couldn't study with friends."

"Any booze around? Or is it BYOB?"

"My mom's got vodka in the freezer," Cam offered. "I can 'borrow' it." Of course he could. His mom swore she had stopped drinking. She couldn't complain if he swiped some of her hidden booze.

Laughing, pushing each other and teasing, they got back into the car. Adam took the highway overpass, looping around for the northbound lanes. But he suddenly slammed on the brakes and pulled onto the shoulder.

"What are you doing?" Cam yelled.

Adam pointed up the road. "Holy shit!"

Far ahead, on the horizon, were clouds so dark it looked like night.

"That storm looks pretty close to home," Adam said. "Should we keep going? Or head back to Harry's and wait it out?"

"Can't we beat it? I've got to be home by four or else," Ava said.

"Your wish is my command, milady," said Adam. Tires squealed as he stepped on the gas and swerved back onto the highway.

In about twenty minutes, they were at the top of a hill. The farmland spread out in front of them was bathed in a weird, yellow-green light.

The dark clouds on the horizon had shape-shifted into a funnel.

Chapter Two

Up ahead cars had slowed, some pulling over. People were getting out of their vehicles to take photos of the tornado that stretched from sky to earth.

"This is so cool!" said Chrissy. "Like in a movie." She stood on the seat and held up her phone, snapping photos.

"Like we're storm chasers," agreed Ava. "Those dudes are seriously crazy."

Adam hit the button for the all-news station on the radio. "...*generators out. Storm over Lake Huron... F3 scale. Police warning all motorists...*" The radio signal crackled on and off. "...*roof collapsed...warning everyone...shelter...*"

F3 scale. Cam felt sick. He knew what that meant. An F3 tornado could be deadly. The measurement scale only went to F5. "We have to go back, Adam," he said. "Drive on the shoulder back to the last exit." He watched Adam thinking, saw him glance in the rearview mirror.

"I can make it to the next exit," Adam answered. "Then we can figure out which way to go." He gunned it, passing the slower-moving cars. He wove in and out, using the shoulder. No cops around to give him a ticket.

In two minutes Cam felt the air turn from hot to cold. And a second later the wind changed. It wasn't just the breeze of driving fast with the roof down. The girls' hair blew straight up. A newspaper and map blew out of the car.

"The roof!" Chrissy yelled. "Adam! Get the roof up!"

Cam could hear the whirring behind his head, and he could see Adam hitting the button for the roof. But the gears weren't cutting it against the wind.

Cam clicked his seat belt open and turned around. He pulled on the edge of the roof. His T-shirt blew up backward over his head, blinding him. He let go of the roof with one hand to yank at his shirt.

Suddenly Cam felt a jolt, as if something had grabbed him and lifted him up. He pushed against the wind, shoving himself down and facing backward on the car floor. His legs were in the air, as if he were an upturned crab.

Ava screamed. Cam saw a stick whack her head, leaving a bloody gash.

He scrambled to get off his back. The funnel shape was closer. They weren't beating the tornado, because the tornado wasn't staying still. It had changed direction and was moving toward them. Touching down, lifting, touching down, lifting, like a kid hopping in a sack race.

Cam screamed in Adam's ear. "Pull over, Adam! Pull over!"

But Adam kept driving like a maniac, his hands clenching the wheel. Chrissy was sobbing, staring straight ahead.

Junk came at them, smashing into the car. A tire, bottles, cans—highway litter was now ammunition.

The sky darkened, and rain fell straight down in pellets as hard as small stones. Along the highway, the tall grasses were flattened.

"Get down!" Cam screamed at Ava. "Like on a plane. Put your head between your legs!"

She nodded and bent over. Then Cam shouted the same direction to Chrissy, but she didn't hear him. He leaned over and grabbed her head, shouting again. She turned to him, her eyes wide open like a deer caught in the headlights. Petrified. But she bent down, tucking under the dash.

Cam put his hands on Adam's shoulders, his mouth at Adam's ear. "Stop!" he screamed. "Pull over! Get off the highway. We have to find a barn or something. Now!" But the wind ripped the words away. He didn't know if Adam had heard him.

The air changed. It felt thick, like they were moving through soup. The rain started to blow sideways.

Cam gripped Adam's headrest. He stared at the monstrous dark funnel, swirling ever closer. A mile away. A minute away. Seconds.

And he knew. He was going to die. They were all going to die.

Ava tugged on his leg, her nails digging into his bare skin. He looked at her and saw the horror on her face. He tried to smile. Wanted so badly to reassure her.

A bomb exploded. Cam heard a horrible sucking sound. The car rose and flipped. He was thrown, whirling, battered. Something hit him on the head and on the chest, arms, legs, back.

He was suffocating. Couldn't breathe. A violent roaring in his ears. Couldn't see. He tried to bring his hands to his head. Couldn't move.

This was death. He was dead. This is what it felt like. Darkness. Noise. Pain.

And gut-wrenching fear.

His body slammed into something.

And then it was over. He was suddenly still. The thundering noise moved farther and farther off. Then it stopped. He could hear wailing and realized the sound was coming from him.

He wasn't dead.

Chapter Three

Cam's hands ached. He brought his fingers to his face and felt something wet. He wiped at his eyes, clenched shut. Slowly, so slowly, he opened them, blinking away the blood.

He was tangled in the low branches of a tree. He tried to move, stretching one leg, then the other, feeling for broken bones. His arms were covered with scratches and cuts. His watch was smashed, the metal band pushed into his flesh. Suddenly he felt himself slip, and he grabbed for a branch. Pain shot up his arm, and he saw his twisted fingers. His head was pounding. He looked down.

Two trees lay on the ground, their huge roots pulled up. Several cars dotted the field, as if a giant's child had been playing with toys. A building—a wooden barn—was missing its roof. Beside it, another building was completely gone. Only the cement foundation was left.

Cam heard screaming. People were moving, crawling. Then he saw the BMW, smashed up against a rock.

"Oh no. Oh god. Oh no. Oh please. Oh no, oh no, oh no," Cam whimpered over and over as he slid and slipped down the tree to the ground. One foot ached. He stared at the ridiculous sight of his feet. He had one shoe on, still laced. The other shoe—gone.

He bent over and clutched his bare foot. A stone was buried deep into his heel. He pulled it out, yelping with pain. He saw a pole to his left. A garden rake. He shoved it into the soil and leaned into it, using it like a crutch.

He began walking. The longest walk of his life. To the car. To the silver BMW, shimmering in the bright sunlight.

Adam was wrapped around the steering wheel. The back of his head was crushed in.

In the back seat, Ava was dead too, her body crumpled, her eyes blank.

Cam threw up. Burger and fries. Still undigested. Because only minutes ago, he was with his friends. And in seconds...

How could it happen? How could...?

Cam retched over and over.

Nightmare. This is a nightmare. I will open my eyes and...

But the screams and moans he could hear in the distance, the shouts, the cries for help from other motorists—Cam knew this was real. The sight of Ava's body, the terror stamped on her face. Adam's fingers tight on the steering wheel.

"Cam." A whisper.

He spun around.

"Help." It was hardly a sound. A bit of breath.

Chrissy. Held tight by her seat belt. She was on the other side of the car, the side that had been only slightly crushed. Cam ran to her. Chrissy was bent over, her head angled back. Her eyes stared at him, pleading.

Cam was afraid to touch her. "Chrissy! Are you okay? Can you tell?"

"I don't…know. Oh, Cam!" She began crying, a hoarse, raspy noise.

He reached in and snapped open the seat belt, then lifted her out of the car. He put her down on the grass, staring at her twisted legs and feet. Her clothes were covered with blood.

He was going to be sick again. He bit back the bile. "I'm going for help. Okay?" He had to get out of here. Get away from his dead friends.

Chrissy grasped at Cam's hand. "Don't leave me. Please. I'm cold, Cam. Cold."

Cam couldn't look at her. And he wanted to pull his hand away. The stench of blood...and worse... "I have to get help. I'll be right back. Promise."

He couldn't do it. Couldn't stay with her. *I can't watch her die.*

Chrissy's eyes fluttered open. "I'm scared," she whispered.

Cam let out a groan. And slowly he reached out his hand. He forced himself to stroke her back. Like he did when Peter had bad dreams and he—

Peter.

Oh no. He was supposed to meet his bus. Dad would kill him.

Cam jumped to his feet, forgetting his cut foot. He groaned, then said, "I have to go! I'll bring help."

Chrissy's eyes were wide open, staring at him blankly.

Cam heard sirens. He looked toward the highway. Police cruisers, fire trucks, ambulances—all heading north. *Why aren't they stopping? Why aren't they stopping here? Helping us?*

He glanced at Chrissy again. At her eyes watching him. Slowly he backed away from her and turned around.

"Hey! Hey!" he shouted, waving his arms. He staggered to the road. Some cars had been spun around by the tornado and looked like they were driving south in the northbound lanes. Other cars were on their sides or upside down, shoved against guardrails. Everywhere people were crying. But it was quiet crying. Like they were too stunned to yell.

Cam limped over to a pickup truck. He could hear the radio through the window. "What's happening?" he asked the driver. "What are they saying?"

"It's over," said the man. "The tornado blew out over Lake of Bays. No damage on the other shore. But up there..." He wiped at his eyes, nodding his chin up the road.

Cam looked up the highway. Blue sky. No clouds. No rain. Sunshine.

"Saying it was an F4. Winds more than 250 miles an hour. Oakwood hit bad. Town's just about gone."

Oakwood gone? And Peter? What happened to Peter? Did he get off his school bus? Is he still waiting for me?

Dizziness flooded Cam's brain. The last thing he saw was the pavement getting closer.

Chapter Four

When Cam came to, he had no idea where he was.

Then it all came back in a rush. Cam heard himself make a sound—a sound like an animal in pain.

"Hey. Hey, kid. Here." The truck driver handed him a bottle of water. "You passed out. I hauled your butt into my truck. I'm heading to Oakwood. Can I take you somewhere?"

"I live there. I've got to get…" Cam trailed off, thinking about Peter. "Is there any more news?"

"I'm getting the police scanner. Nothing but bad. Just about everything's destroyed. Houses, the whole mall. Local high school's gone. Flattened. All the portables sucked up. But not a lot of casualties. The students were let out early."

Lucky.

"What about—what about Oakwood Primary?"

The driver shook his head. "I don't know."

Cam stared out the window.

"Name's Dave," said the man. "You?"

"Cam. Cam Mitchell. My parents work in Millbrook. At a factory. Have you heard anything about Millbrook?"

"Oakwood was the center, that's all I know. Don't know what else has been hit yet."

Cam heard sirens. Two army trucks veered off the shoulder and drove across the field. *They'll find them. They'll find Ava and Adam. And Chrissy.*

They'll help Chrissy. They don't need me. I don't have to go back there.

Two huge tow trucks passed on the shoulder. They stopped up ahead, beside some police cruisers. Cam could see cops checking out a car that was upside down. Someone stuck his arm out of the car window, and a cop kneeled down on the highway.

"Rescue's gonna be a humdinger," Dave muttered.

A policeman thumped on the hood of the pickup. "We're moving everyone we can off the road. Let's go!"

They pulled out slowly and joined a long line of vehicles heading north. The road and fields were covered in wood, bricks, shingles. Cam saw a spot where the guardrail dividing the north and south lanes was missing. Then he saw it wrapped around a tree. Like a kid had taken a roll of tinfoil and decorated the trunk.

They passed the racetrack, and Dave swore. The buildings were smashed apart, horses flung over the grass. Dead. Piles of manure lined the highway.

But on the other side of the highway—nothing. Like another world. The buildings were all intact. The trees were standing tall. Cows were grazing.

And if we had been on that side, we'd be fine. We'd all be fine. Alive.

Cam looked at his swollen hand. Two fingers broken for sure.

"Two of my friends are dead. Back there. The other one...I left her. She was still alive, but I left her lying there. She couldn't walk and..."

Dave didn't speak.

The pounding in Cam's head was worse. "And I have to get home. My brother, he's six, and he's waiting for me at the bus stop. He's...Peter. His name is Peter, and he's..."

Cam shoved his hands, balled into fists, into his eyes. "I shouldn't have gone with them. I shouldn't have...but we got let out early. Power went off. And so... and so—"

"Listen to me," said Dave. "This isn't your fault. There isn't a warning with a tornado. Or not much of one. No rules. They're saying it was a blessing the school got let out. Saved all your lives."

Cam slumped in his seat and closed his eyes. He couldn't keep them open anymore. He couldn't look at this highway dividing the living from the dead. One side perfect—like his life one hour ago. The other side demolished—his life this minute.

The truck stopped. Cam opened his eyes. A police officer was waving drivers off the road at exit 10.

"What's going on?" Dave asked. "I'm going to Oakwood."

"No, sir. We're not letting anyone past this point. Power lines are down. Gas mains are—"

"I got family there! This kid lives there. We're not sightseeing!"

The police officer didn't react. "Yes, sir. We understand. But no one is allowed past this mark.

Follow the cars in front, and turn off the highway. There's an information center set up in Bayville. Check in there."

Dave grumbled, but he turned off at the exit. Several army vehicles zoomed past, going north.

"Don't worry, kid. I've lived in these parts all my life." He made a sharp left onto a dirt road. The other cars kept going. "Okay, Cam. I don't know what's up ahead, but we're going to find out. Not letting cops keep me from seeing my family."

They bumped along the badly rutted road, bouncing up and down in their seats. Dave stopped the truck at a Christmas-tree farm. All the pines were snapped in half, their tops missing. Just jagged spikes, row on row, left in the ground. The earth looked like giant gophers had churned it up.

"How could this happen?" Dave asked. "How could..."

Cam hung on as Dave turned left, right, left through the fields. He was taking roads that looked more like cow paths. And the farther they got from the highway, the less damage they saw.

But then they climbed a hill on the east side of Oakwood. Dave slowed to a stop, and they both stared.

Destruction. Like something Cam had seen only in movies. Or games—war games. The wide path of the tornado zigzagged through town. Here and there, some buildings were untouched. The road in front of them was covered in rubble.

Dave opened his door. "We'll have to leave the truck here and walk in. My folks' place is on the other side of the mall. That's where I'm heading."

Cam got out, wincing as he put pressure on his bad foot. He stood for a moment, holding on to the door. He didn't want to move. He didn't want to find out. As long as he was in the truck, he was safe from knowing the worst. As long as they were driving, he was in a time warp—a little safe space between the past and the future.

Dave came around to Cam's side, holding out a pair of old construction boots. "You can't walk through that mess without shoes. These should fit."

Cam nodded and sat down. He pulled off his one shoe and tugged on the boots.

"Ready?" Dave reached down a hand. "Come on, kid. Time to be a man."

Cam suddenly thought of Ava. Remembered how many times she called him "my man." He saw her terrified face again, her broken body.

A million years ago.

He took Dave's hand and pulled himself up. He was crying, and he didn't care. He didn't want to be a man. He wanted to be a little boy and find his mommy and cry himself to sleep.

Dave put his arm around him. "Look. I don't know what all happened to you back there. But you're alive, and you're needed. You gotta think about what you can do to help. You can feel sorry for yourself some other time."

Cam wiped his face with his shirt and blew his nose. The jackhammer in his skull was worse.

He's right. I have to find out. Have to find Peter.

"Thanks," Cam mumbled. He pointed to his left. "Peter's school is over there. I'll start there." He closed the truck door. "Dave—thanks for...for getting me here. I mean it. I—thanks."

"Yup. Good luck, Cam. See you around."

Cam turned and walked down the hill to Oakwood Primary School.

The little time warp had come to an end.

Chapter Five

The school was still standing. Not damaged at all. No broken windows or missing roof. The swings and slides looked ready for kids to rush out and play on.

For a moment—a wonderful, crazy moment—Cam thought the nightmare was over. And now he was awake.

Except...

On the other side of the street, the houses were gone. Bricks and shingles and glass smashed. Pulverized. Trees torn out of the ground. One house still had a wall with stairs going up to nothing. The second floor wasn't there. People were picking through the rubble. Sirens blared in the distance.

But over there—Cam stared at the tulips. *How did flowers survive?*

Cam felt hope. Peter was okay, he thought. All the kids were okay. Of course. When the school heard the news, they kept the kids safe. Kept them in the gym, out of danger. Of course!

"Cam?"

He spun around.

"Cam? Oh my goodness! You look terrible! What are you doing here?"

"Miss Chang. I…" Cam didn't know what to say to his fourth-grade teacher. "I was down the highway. Some of my friends…we didn't…" He took a deep breath. "I'm here for Peter. Where are the kids?"

"All the children left on the buses before we knew about the tornado. After that—" Her face crumpled. "After that, I don't know what happened to them. When we saw the funnel, we—the staff—we ran to the basement to wait it out. I'm the only one still here. The others have gone home. Or, well, to find out the worst."

Peter got on the bus. Cam didn't listen to anything else Miss Chang said. He walked away as fast as he could. Didn't care about the pain in his foot.

He followed the route the bus usually took to drop off the kids. And everywhere he saw the same things. One house still standing, untouched, the next house destroyed. Cam remembered the way the tornado had hopped. If it hopped over your house, lucky you. But then it touched down again. And if that was your house? Too bad, sucker. Everything you owned—gone.

Oakwood was like a ghost town. There was hardly anyone around. Cam figured the army was relocating people. The few people he saw walking the streets seemed numb. And when he asked, no one remembered seeing the school bus.

"I was in the basement, doing laundry," one woman said. "And if not for that...well..." She looked at the ruins of her house. "Well, I guess I'd be dead." Tears ran down her face, and she didn't bother to wipe them away.

Cam kept going. He limped along the road that headed out of town. He passed the first field and saw rows of young corn. And someone's sofa plunked down in the middle of them.

"Hey, Cam-Cammy!"

Cam stopped short. The yellow house, Sammy Khan's house, was still there, looking as perfect as it always did. *Peter got off the bus with his best buddy. Of course. He is here. He is waiting out the storm here.*

For once he didn't mind Peter's best friend calling him Cammy.

He answered the usual way. "Hey, Sam-Sammy!"

Sammy ran to hug him. "Where's Peter?" Sammy asked.

And all of Cam's hopes crashed.

"I...I don't know. I haven't been home yet," he said, looking down at Peter's little friend. "But he was on the bus with you, right? Was he okay?"

"We was scared, Cammy. We both was. But Peter fibbed and said he wasn't. He said you'd be waiting for him. He wanted to go home."

Just then Sammy's dad came around the corner with a wheelbarrow. "You okay, Cam? Lucky you kids got out of school early. How are your folks?" Sammy's dad didn't wait for an answer. "Check this out," he said, pointing to the wheelbarrow. It was filled with all sorts of things—a toaster, books, a broken lamp. "This crap all landed in the yard. Who knows how far it traveled."

Cam was too agitated to have any kind of normal conversation. "I'm sorry, Mr. Khan, I have to go. I haven't been home yet."

Sammy's dad looked puzzled. "Where's Peter?"

Cam stared at Sammy's dad, who had his arm around his son. The anger surged again. "Why didn't you keep him with you? Why didn't you get Peter off the bus? He was scared. Why didn't you tell him to stay with you? To—"

"Hey, now wait a minute, Cam," Sammy's dad said. "I know you're stressed out, and it's natural to want to blame someone. But I didn't know there was a tornado coming. And I didn't know you weren't at home."

Cam was moving backward now, back out to the road, pretending he didn't hear.

Blame. He didn't want to think about that word.

If the teachers had kept the kids at school. *If* Peter had stayed with Sammy. Then he would be off the hook. *Yeah, sure, Cam. And if you hadn't taken off with your friends...*

Cam slammed his fist into his forehead. *Shut up. Shut up. Shut up.*

Cam kept walking. Past the Singh farm. Off the main road. Over the bridge. When trees blocked his path, Cam had to climb over them if he couldn't go around. A smashed rowboat lay in the middle of Spruce Lane, and Cam wondered where it had come from. This road was a couple of miles from the lake.

Just as his house came into view, Cam stopped and stared down at his feet. He was afraid to look.

A siren sounded somewhere. It was like a wake-up call, and Cam raised his head.

His house was split down the middle. Half of it was still standing. The walls for the other half weren't there. Cam saw his parents out front. The lawn was covered with busted-up chunks of building materials. A bed lay upside down in the strawberry patch. His parents were bent over, picking through the litter. He could see that his mom was holding a kettle in her hand. Cam felt hysterical. *Tea? You're going to make tea?*

Relief swamped him, flushing away the anger. They were safe. Alive. Cam wanted to run to them. Hug them. Forget about all the fights. But...*where was Peter?*

Suddenly it all made sense to Cam. He knew. It was like some cruel game of "Eenie, Meenie, Miney, Mo." He was safe. His friends weren't. His parents were safe. And his brother? Like his house, he and his brother would be split apart. There was no way—no way—that he and his brother were both alive. One of them had to pay the price.

Just then Cam's mom looked up and saw him. She put her hand to her eyes to cut the glare of the sun. "Cam?" she said, her voice shaky.

Then she was running. Hopping over the crap on the lawn. "Cam! Cam! Cam, Cam." She said it over and over until she was holding him, sobbing. "What happened to you? Look at you! What happened?"

He didn't answer. He wanted to stay like this forever. He wanted to feel his mom's arms around him, squeezing him. The way she used to do before all the fighting started. Before she started picking on him almost every day.

Cam hugged her back, and then his dad was there, his arms around them both.

It was one perfect moment. One perfect *last* moment. Because, of course...

"Where's Peter?" his dad asked.

Cam opened his mouth. And shut it. His body went cold. Something felt hard in his chest. He knew what would happen if he told the truth.

"What do you mean? I told him to stay here," Cam lied. "I told him to wait right here and not move. I went to...to help." Cam broke away from his parents. "What are you saying? Are you saying Peter isn't here?" He looked around frantically, acting his ass off. *Don't overdo it, idiot!*

He ran, limping, toward the house.

"Cam! Stop! It isn't safe! Don't go inside!" his mom yelled.

Cam ignored her. Up the steps and through the gap that used to be the front door. He stopped, staring. The washer and dryer from the basement were in the living room. Sucked up through the huge hole in the floor.

He forced himself to walk down the hallway. On one side, his bedroom looked almost like he had left it that morning. On the other side, Peter's bedroom was a wreck. Except for his closet. The door was missing, but Peter's clothes still hung on hangers.

Cam stepped over the rubble. Was Peter in here? Did he wait for Cam and then run inside? Hide under the bed? Peter was afraid of storms. He always crawled under his bed when he heard thunder.

Plaster, wooden beams, bricks and glass had fallen. The bed was flattened.

Then he saw it. Peter's backpack. Just the corner of it, sticking out from under the bed.

A little kid's superhero backpack.

Chapter Six

His parents were coming. Shouting his name. No time to think. What lie to tell? Cam had to think fast. He kicked a piece of plaster to cover up the backpack and turned around.

"I'm going to go looking for Peter. I told him to stay in the yard. I told him not to move. He must have—he must have followed me."

Cam saw the look on his dad's face. Questioning. Wondering.

His dad raised his hand. "Okay. Back it up. I don't quite understand. Exactly where were you when the tornado hit?" he asked.

Stupid! Why didn't I think this through? "I, uh, I…" The answer was suddenly there in his mind, ready for him. "I was here, waiting for the bus. I could see a storm coming, and I got Peter, and we…we hid in the basement. It was terrible. It…"

Cam covered his eyes with his hands. "I don't know why Peter didn't listen to me."

"What happened to your fingers?" his mom asked.

"I tried to help some people. They…uh…they were calling for help. And I…after I made sure Peter was okay, I went to see if I could do anything. I didn't want to leave Peter, but they were…trapped. And I helped pull them out and…my fingers…" Cam held up his hand like he was just noticing the damage for the first time. "Jeez."

"Thank goodness you're okay, Cam," his mom said.

Cam wanted to stay. Wanted to enjoy this moment—his mom and dad thinking he was a hero. But he had to get his parents out of this area so he could search it properly. He stepped away from the wreck of Peter's room and entered his own.

His dad followed him and said, "Where would he go? If you told him to stay here, where did he go? Would he have run to Sammy's house?" His dad didn't wait for an answer. "That makes sense. I'll see what I can find out."

"Cam..." His mom didn't finish whatever she was going to say. She hurried after her husband.

Cam looked around his room. So weird. He could sleep here tonight, if he wanted to. A few books were on the floor, and some stuff had fallen off shelves. At the window Cam waited until he could see his parents outside. Then he rushed back to his brother's room.

He dropped to his knees and dug through the crap. He pushed everything under the bed out of the way. Then, groaning at its weight, Cam managed to lift the bed a little bit off the floor. He forced a chair leg under and then got down on his stomach to look.

Nothing.

Relieved, Cam scrambled to his feet. *So he came here to hide. But then what? Did something scare him? Did he run outside when the storm hit?* It didn't matter what had happened. Peter wasn't dead. At least, not as far as Cam knew. He had to find him.

His fingers were aching. He went into the bathroom—what was left of it. The toilet was on its side, the tub pulled away from the wall. Without thinking, he turned on the tap, holding his hands under the faucet. When no water came out, it took Cam a moment to understand.

Everything had changed. Nothing would ever be the same.

He got a look at himself in the broken mirror. Cuts and scratches on his face, streaks of vomit on his shirt. Three buttons torn off. Part of his eyebrow missing. His hair was matted with blood. But he was alive. Because he had been thrown out of the car and lived. The others—

Stop, stop, stop, stop! There's nothing I can do about them. Find Peter. That's what I can do. Find Peter.

Cam walked to the back of the house and stepped over some loose bricks. His foot slipped on a chunk of drywall, and he reached out wildly for where the door should have been. He landed hard on his butt, and something poked him in the thigh. He scrambled up and saw a nail jutting out of the floorboard. In a normal world, his mom would be hauling him off for a tetanus shot. *But we are no longer in a normal world.*

He moved more carefully until he was away from the house.

Where would Peter go? Where would he hide?

The shed at the back of the yard was still standing. The door was unlatched, but it shouldn't be. Cam felt his heart racing as he pushed open the door. When it was halfway open, he heard something scraping along the floor. "Peter?" He waited for his eyes to adjust to the gloom. "Peter? You in here?"

He shoved aside garden stuff. Looked behind the snow blower. Nothing. Looked inside the rain barrel they had bought and never used. Pushed at the pile of shovels and rakes.

There was dust and dirt on everything. The lawn mower was where he had left it the previous week. But—beside it was a wet spot.

Cam bent over and touched it. Not oil. Water? He smelled his finger. *Urine?* He bent down, nose close to the floor, and inhaled. *He was here! Had to be! He hid here and was so scared he pissed his pants!*

But why had he left? The shed was still standing. Nothing was destroyed. Why leave a safe place? Cam noticed a clay pot pulled out from the wall, and in a second he'd added up the clues. *That's what I heard when I opened the door. It was behind the door, and I pushed it. And it was there because Peter stood on it to look out the only window. And he saw—he saw the tornado! He saw it coming toward him. And he ran. Ran where? Probably as far in the opposite direction as he could.*

Cam left the shed and hurried to the hedge. It was thick and covered with thorns. But he spotted something bright red on the ground just inside the brambles. And Cam knew what it was. He shoved his arm through and grabbed on to Peter's favorite action figure, Spider-Man. And he remembered the day he'd bought it for Peter.

"Spider-Man? Seriously? But you're afraid of spiders, Peter!" Cam laughed at his little brother. "You scream when you see a daddy longlegs."

"Spider-Man makes me not afraid, Cammy."

"Spider-Man got bit by a spider. I mean, Peter Parker did. You'd cry like a baby if you got bit."

"But I'd get superpower. If I got bit. Because I'm Peter too. And I wouldn't be afraid of nothing ever, ever again."

Cam smiled at his brother and got out his wallet. Go figure. Only six years old, and he stood up to what scared him most. "Happy birthday, buddy."

Cam gripped the toy. What had made Peter drop it? It was his good-luck charm. And so far it had worked. Peter hadn't been killed hiding under the bed. The tornado hadn't damaged the shed or the hedge. So—

"Cam! Cam, where are you?"

His mom. He started to shout back a reply, but then he saw the car in the driveway. The black BMW. The other one that belonged to Adam's father.

And Adam's parents were talking to his mom and dad.

Before he could move, before he could hide, his dad spotted him and yelled.

Cam saw the look on his dad's face. Furious.

Chapter Seven

If Cam ran, shoved through the hedge and ran, how long before they caught up to him? And then what? Did Adam's parents know the truth? Did they know their son was dead? And if he ran now, what would they think? Would they blame him somehow?

Cam realized his whole body was shaking. *Not your fault, kid,* he remembered Dave telling him. He took a deep breath. *It isn't my fault. None of it.*

Not the tornado, not the deaths. And so what if I went out for burgers with my friends? I had planned to get home for Peter. I had!

He walked around to the front yard. *What could his mom say in front of Adam's parents? "I told you not to hang out with that spoiled brat"? Yeah, right.*

When Cam reached his mom's side, he stopped. He said nothing and waited.

"Gosh, Cam! What the hell happened to you?" Mr. Brown asked. "We heard you were with Adam, and we don't know where he is or what happened. We're hoping you can tell us."

Oh no. They don't know.

"Some kids at school saw you get in the car with him," Adam's mom added. "You and Chrissy and Ava. Where did you go? Where are they now? Nobody has seen them. Ava and Chrissy's parents are worried sick too."

Cam swallowed. He ran his tongue over his lips and tasted dried blood.

"Look, Cam. We know the school shut down early. So where did you go? Just walk us through it." Adam's dad sounded so calm.

Cam looked away. "We, uh, we got out early. And we...Adam said he was going for burgers, and so we—"

"Where?" Adam's mom demanded. "And if you tell me he drove to Halton..."

Cam didn't answer. Adam had said he was only allowed to take the BMW out on the highway if one of his parents was with him.

"I'm right, aren't I? You all went to Halton?"

Cam nodded. "Yeah. We went to Harry's. On the way back, we...we saw the tornado and..." He wondered how much to tell them. All of it? Some of it? "We tried to pull over. Get off the road to safety. But—" He had to stop. He was shaking.

"And? What happened?" Adam's mom's voice rose in a shriek.

Cam swallowed the sick taste in his mouth. He couldn't look at either of Adam's parents. "And...then it was just there. The tornado. We got...I think we got... pulled into it. I couldn't see...couldn't.....I got thrown out of the car."

Adam's mom began to sob.

"Where? Where were you?" Adam's dad demanded. "Where did this happen?"

"South of exit 10." Cam put his hand to his head. Felt the crusty blood. "That's all I remember."

"But Adam? The girls? What happened? You must remember something more!"

I left them dead in a field. Chrissy was alive, but I left her there to die.

He couldn't do it. Couldn't tell them the truth. "I don't know what happened to them. Some guy found me on the side of the road. He got me into his truck, and I passed out. When I came to, we were here. In Oakwood. I was messed up, confused. I just wanted to come home." Cam finally looked at Adam's parents directly. "I'm sorry. I don't know where they are now."

"Wait a minute," said Cam's dad. His face looked like thunder. "Are you saying you *weren't* here when Peter got off the bus? You *lied* to us?"

Cam saw his dad's fists tighten. And something blew up in him. He stopped shaking, and his body felt hard. "Yeah!" he shouted. "I lied! Okay? I lied! Because I knew how this would go! And what about me? I got sucked up in a tornado. Do either of you even care?" Cam heard his voice catch. Heard the sob. "I almost died. But all I could think about was making sure my little brother was okay."

His mom didn't move. Didn't reach out for him, pull him close. His dad just stood there, motionless too. *I don't care anymore.* Cam turned to Adam's parents. Mr. Brown was trying to make a call on his cell but wasn't getting through.

Cam looked at Adam's mom. "I lied because they"—he jerked his thumb at his mom and dad—"they don't want me hanging around with Adam. They think he's trouble."

Cam's mom's jaw dropped. She twirled around to look at Adam's mom. "No. Cathy. No. That's not true. I never, I would never say such a—"

"Go to hell, all of you," Mr. Brown said, pulling his wife back to the car. They both climbed in and slammed their doors.

Cam watched them pull away. They swerved around some rubble on the road, and Cam saw a green army jeep stop on the shoulder. He waited, wondering if now was when he was going to get caught. Caught for telling the really big lie.

A man climbed out and waved. "You folks okay?" he called. "We're checking for anyone who needs medical attention. We've got a triage station set up at the barracks over in Bolton."

Cam's mom rushed toward him. "My son is missing! We don't know where he is! Please help. Help us, please!" She described Peter.

"We've got a whole unit out searching for missing

persons. The Red Cross has started a list. Their station is at All Saints Church."

Cam waited for his parents to say something about him. When they didn't bother, he called out, "Yeah, I'm hurt. I was on the highway by exit 10. I was thrown out of a car." He held up his hands. "I got slammed into a tree. I think one of my fingers is broken."

"What's your name?"

"Cam. Cam Mitchell."

"Well, Cam, sounds like you've got a great story to tell one day, son." The man smiled at him and then glanced at his parents. "You should get him checked for concussion. Shock too."

"Thanks. We'll handle it," his dad replied.

"We've got supplies coming in from all over the county. Oakwood Primary has been turned into a shelter for sleeping. You can get water and food, blankets."

His mom mumbled, "Thank you."

The man climbed back into the jeep and drove down the road to the next house.

Cam stood still. Waited for his parents to start shouting at him.

Nothing. Cam finally turned around. His mom was standing in the vegetable patch, as still as a scarecrow. She was just staring.

He heard the slam of the pickup's door. Saw his dad plow across what was left of the driveway.

As the truck got close to Cam, his dad stuck his head out the window. "I'm going to Sammy's," he said. "They didn't answer before when I called. I want to make sure Peter was on the bus."

Tell the truth. "He was on the bus," Cam said. *Why can't I just tell the truth?* "He came here. Mr. Khan said so. I checked."

"So he was here *alone*?" The pain on his dad's face was unbearable.

Cam reached out his hand. "Dad," he choked out. "Dad, I'm sorry. I really am. I..."

His dad put the truck in gear. "It's time you were told the truth. I'm not your dad. You're not my son." He gestured toward the garden in disgust. "Ask the drunk back there."

Chapter Eight

Cam stared as the truck bumped its way to the road. *Not your son?* He looked over at his mom, wondering if she had heard.

She was bent over, shoving some bricks aside. She stood up, a piece of a broken plate in each hand. She joined them together, nodding.

Junk. She's putting together broken junk, thinking it can be fixed. Whole again.

If what his dad said was true, then they'd never be whole again. *Just like that stupid plate.*

He walked over to his mom. "Is it true? What he said? Is it, Mom?"

"Not now, Cam. Can't you see I'm busy? Lots to do around here. Peter will be home soon. Got to make dinner."

What is she talking about? Cam grabbed the plate pieces and smashed them on the ground. "Who cares about this crap?" he yelled. She wouldn't look at him. "Mom! Who cares?" And when she still didn't look up, Cam reached out and shook her.

She went limp in his arms. "A year ago. He found out a year ago. I was young. Stupid. A mistake. Was never going to tell him. And I didn't. But a year ago—" She started crying. "My mistake showed up at the bar one night. Talked about me. And, well…"

A year ago. End of tenth grade. That's when it started. The fighting. The look in Dad's eyes. And Mom drinking.

She sobbed, "I'm sorry. Oh, Cam, I truly am. And now this." She flung her arms wide. "All this. And Peter missing. It's all my fault. I brought this on."

He wanted to tell her she was crazy, but he couldn't. *Don't I feel the same way? Isn't Peter being missing my fault?* "Mom, I can't—I can't deal with this right now. I have to look for Peter. I have to." He walked away from his mom and around to the rear of the house, back to the spot where he'd found the Spider-Man action figure.

A sudden urge came over him. He wanted to call Ava, tell her everything. Let her put her arms around him. Kiss him. But what about all the lies he'd told? What would she think of him? *My whole life is a lie. I'm a lie. I don't even know who I am.* He wanted to run to his bedroom and crawl under the covers. Forget everything.

And who the hell is my dad? My real dad?

His head was going to explode. *Should have been me. Back there in the BMW. I wish it had been me. But Peter...*

Cam forced himself to think only about Peter. Where would a six-year-old go if he saw a tornado coming? Cam got down on his knees in front of the hedge, which made him about the same height as Peter. Now he could just barely see over the hedge. He looked to his left, in the direction of the ditch. The water from the creek was surging, flooding the ditch with stormwater now.

Cam jumped up. Of course. Of course! He knew where Peter would go! There was hardly a trickle of water in that ditch most days. It had been one of Peter's favorite hiding places when they played hide-and-seek. He would often lie flat in the hollow of the dry ditch, thinking no one could see him there.

Cam scrambled through the bushes. Thorns caught at his clothes. *That's what happened! Peter didn't drop Spider-Man. It got ripped out of his pocket.* Cam knew he was on the right track. He burst through the bushes and ran across the field, then stumbled and skidded down the side of the ditch.

The water, muddy and fast, swirled about his thighs. It was full of junk—roof shingles, pieces of wood, a dead cat. Cam stopped for a moment. The cat's eyes were staring. Cam noticed the collar and tag. Someone's pet.

Cam looked toward the overflow pipe. It was still gated, but the bars were far enough apart for someone small to squeeze through. *Did Peter try that? Did he think hiding in the pipe would protect him?*

The water was gushing through the opening. *Oh no. Oh please no.* Because Peter couldn't have survived that. No one could. Cam waded upstream until he was right next to the pipe. He saw something pressed against the gate. A face.

His stomach heaved. But then he realized it was a doll, its creepy smile squashed against the bars.

"Peter! Peter!" Cam screamed. He had to assume Peter had kept going. Cam grabbed for the weeds on the bank to keep from sliding in the mud. *Now think like Peter. Where would he go? How far did he get?*

Not far, Cam was sure. Peter had wanted to hide, not run. Cam willed himself to take a deep breath. Willed himself to calm down. *Think!* If Peter hadn't been swept away, then he must still be nearby. Cam stared at the opposite bank. He shielded his eyes from the sun, low on the horizon now. And for a moment, he was confused.

The sun. It was still the same day. Only hours had passed since the tornado. But it felt like days and days. What time was it anyway? It was the middle of June, so maybe eight or nine o'clock.

Cam started looking again, moving his eyes slowly over every bit of bank. One side, then the other. Nothing. He plunged back into the middle of the water, forcing his way to the opposite side. It wasn't far—only a few steps—but the water shoved hard at his knees.

With the sun behind him, he could see the other bank clearly. And—there! His heart lurched. A pile of clothes. Caught in the bend near a huge willow tree.

Cam clutched at the weeds and yanked himself along. More debris floated by, banging into him. A lawn chair. A sun umbrella.

He made it to the giant tree on the edge of the bank. Some of its exposed roots reached down into the water. Cam reached out and grabbed at the tangled pile. It was a clothesline. A clothesline with towels and sheets, caught on the roots.

Cam wanted to howl. He had been so sure he was about to find another clue. So certain. Furious, he yanked at the pile again, and the line pulled free. He watched the clothing float away, unsure what he should do next. A drip from the tree above him made him look up. He spotted a familiar flash of blue and red.

A Spider-Man shirt.

Chapter Nine

When Cam spotted the body curled up in the roots of the willow tree, his heart sank.

Peter's face was upturned, eyes closed. His fingers were buried deep into the mud surrounding the roots.

Cam scrambled up the side of the ditch, trying not to slip and fall. He grabbed his brother's shoulders. "Peter!" he screamed. "Come on, Peter. Wake up!"

Cam pried his brother's fingers loose and scooped him into his arms. He shoved his hand in under Peter's shirt. Placed his hand on Peter's heart. He held his own breath.

He felt Peter's heart beating. Not dead! Peter wasn't dead!

His brother's head flopped backward, and Cam cupped his hand behind it. Peter's eyes fluttered open.

"Knew you'd find me, Cammy," whispered Peter.

Cam felt his throat tighten. "You can't beat me at hide-and-seek, little man." He pulled him closer.

"I was scared."

"Me too."

Cam thought hard. Should he go back home? His dad was out in the truck. And his mom? Useless. He needed to get Peter to a hospital. He was closer to the main road from here. Maybe he could get there and flag someone down.

Cam walked across the field, stepping carefully. The sun was almost down, and the ground was littered with trash. Every few steps he wobbled, like he'd just gotten off the Whirl-A-Twirl at the local fair. His foot felt something soft, and he heard a faint yelp. He moved back and peered down. Under a hunk of wood, he spotted an injured dog, its eyes begging.

Cam covered his brother's eyes so he wouldn't see Patch, their neighbor's collie. He lifted the wood with his toe, and when he saw the rest of the animal's body, he knew there was nothing he could do.

And so he walked away. *Just like I did with Chrissy.* Because Cam knew that if he didn't, if he sat down by that mangled dog, he would never get up. He was so exhausted. Every cell in his body was screaming at him to stop. But his brother needed him. Cam shifted Peter's weight. Normally he could carry his little brother effortlessly, but now it was all he could do to keep going. The sun had set now, and in the twilight Cam could barely see. *If I trip, if I stumble and fall...* He took a deep breath and moved east across the field, into the darkness toward the Martellos' house.

The house was demolished. Cam called out anyway. Maybe someone was still around. Maybe someone could give them a ride. But no one shouted back. Cam thought briefly that the Martellos might be injured. That maybe he should check through the rubble. But he had to stay focused. He had to get help for his brother.

Your *half brother*, something ugly whispered in his mind.

Cam kept walking.

The road was deserted. No cars passing. No streetlights out here on the back roads. Cam realized he was being stupid. *No lights anywhere, moron. No electricity.* "Okay if I move you, Peter? Put you on my back?" He didn't wait for an answer. He knelt down and put Peter on the pavement. Then he hoisted him around and onto his back, tucking in Peter's legs and holding his hands. "That's better. Now I can go for miles." He tried to sound strong. He didn't want his brother to see how close he was to collapsing.

"I saw it coming, Cammy," Peter said. "I saw the tomato."

"You—you saw the *tomato*? Really?" And Cam couldn't help it. He started laughing. Small noises, then louder, until he was laughing so hard the tears came.

"Did I make a funny, Cammy? Did I?"

Cam caught his breath. "It's not a tomato, it's a *tornado*, dummy!" He clasped both of Peter's wrists in his right hand and used his left to wipe his eyes. He felt the throbbing in his fingers, and as quick as that, nothing was funny anymore.

Peter was silent for a moment. "I was really scared, Cammy."

"I know, little man. I'm sorry I wasn't there when you got off the bus."

Peter nodded. "Yeah. I gots off the bus and you weren't there and the bus drove away."

And you could have died. Again Cam felt sick. About what could have happened. And about what did happen.

He was almost at the main road. Above him, search beams crisscrossed the night sky. A jeep drove by, not spotting them. It was past before Cam could wave it down.

"Can we go home, Cammy? Can we? I'm hungry, and I want Mommy."

"I know, I know. But..." *What can I tell him?* "Sorry, kid, we don't have a home and Mommy is a zombie"? *And, oh yeah,* "Dad hates my guts"? "We'll go home, don't worry. But first we have to get to a hospital."

"I don't like hospitals." Peter started to squirm, trying to get down off Cam's back.

"Not for you, dummy! For me. I was hurt real bad, Peter."

Peter stopped wiggling and kissed the back of Cam's neck. A big, sloppy, little-kid smack. "I'm sorry you got hurt, Cammy."

If I cry one more time today...

Cam could see the small shopping plaza and a pickup truck out front. Its headlights were on, beaming at a store.

Help. Finally. We'll get help.

He walked into Done Deal—or what used to be Done Deal. All its windows were blown out. A steel girder in one corner had buckled. But the roof and walls still held. Two people were inside, pulling things off shelves, shoving stuff in duffel bags.

"Hey! Can you help us? We need to get to a hospital."

The two men turned around. Faces covered.

And one of them was pointing a gun right at Cam.

Chapter Ten

"Get down on the floor! Down!" The guy with the gun waved it angrily.

Cam froze.

"Now!" the man yelled.

Cam stumbled to his knees. Peter slipped from his back.

"You too! On the floor! Don't move."

Peter stood there, frozen. Cam pulled him to his side, his arm around him. "Close your eyes," he whispered.

"Shut up!" the man screamed. "No talking!"

Cam could hear the other man still tossing stuff into the bags.

"Let's go," the man with the gun said. "There may be other people around."

Then the other man spoke. "What if he saw our plates?"

"You think I'm killing someone for a bunch of electronics? You nuts?"

"Then tie them up. Shove them in the basement. Maybe the place will collapse on them."

"Forget it, man. Let's get out of here."

Cam felt Peter shaking. He hugged him tighter.

The men swore at each other, but they moved toward the doorway. As they left, one of them smashed something on the floor. Cam jerked.

Don't move. Don't breathe.

Cam kept his head down until he heard the engine revving. Tires squealing. *Not yet. Don't move.*

He counted to ten. Then everything went dark.

"Cammy? You asleep? You okay?"

Cam rolled over and sat up. His vision seemed so blurry. Peter crawled into his lap.

"They were bad men, weren't they, huh, Cammy?"

"Yup. Looters. They were stealing stuff." To Cam's surprise, Peter grinned.

"Just like in a comic book, Cammy. Crooks and everything."

Cam nodded. "Yup. A comic book. You nailed it."

"And you're the superhero. Super Brother!"

Super half brother.

He managed to smile. "You hungry, little man? There's lots of stuff to eat in here. Let's look around."

When Peter jumped up and ran to the counter, Cam was shocked. His brother wasn't hurt. "Hey!

You been faking me? I thought you had a broken leg or something."

Peter looked down at his legs. "Nope."

"So why did I have to carry you, huh?" Cam teased. "You're a lazy sack of—" Cam blinked. There were two Peters in front of him. *I'm seeing double.* He rubbed his eyes. *Tired. So tired. That's all.*

"I thought you was carrying me 'cause I don't have shoes on my feets."

"Yup. That's why, all right." Cam moved toward the candy section. He lost his balance and veered to one side. *It feels like I'm drunk.* He forced himself to walk straight. "What do you want, Peter?" he called out. "Chips? Chocolate bars?" He grabbed two cans of soda and reached for the large bag of Doritos.

Suddenly the store was flooded with light.

"Drop it." A stern command.

Cam dropped the cans. He squinted into the light but was blinded. His head swam.

"Cammy!" Peter wailed. "Are the bad men back?"

"It's a kid. A couple of kids," said someone from behind the light.

When the man lowered the light, Cam could see he was wearing a uniform. Army.

"We—we didn't do this," stuttered Cam. "We saw the looters. They had a gun. We—" He grabbed for Peter's hand.

"Okay. Okay. Easy does it. Tell us who you are and what happened."

Weakness suddenly flooded Cam's body. So dizzy. Cam leaned into the counter. He knew he was falling. Two young men—cadets—caught him and dragged him over to a bench. Cam told them his story.

Someone ordered them all into the truck parked outside. As he settled into his seat beside Peter, Cam felt safe for the first time. Someone was taking charge of him. He could stop being Super Brother.

They drove along the road out to the highway, swerving around rubble. Cam leaned his head against the window, trying to figure out where they were heading.

One of the cadets spoke. "We're taking you to the barracks in Bolton. A doctor will check you out. Anyone with serious injuries will be airlifted to City Hospital."

Cam nodded. He was mesmerized by the couple of wispy hairs on the cadet's chin. *He's not even shaving. Yet he sounds so sure of himself.*

They drove for a few more minutes in the dark. Then Cam saw streetlights and store lights blazing. None of the buildings they passed were damaged. The truck turned off the main road and stopped at a checkpoint. They were waved through to the grounds of the barracks.

The young cadet helped Cam to his feet. "I can't shhtand. I mean, shh...shh..." *Why am I slurring?*

The cadet leaned in toward Cam, breathing deeply. "Had a few, did you?"

What? Oh! He thinks I'm drunk!

They entered the huge building. The cadet was still holding Cam up. Peter clung tightly to Cam's other hand.

Cam was shocked by what he saw. Dozens of people lying on stretchers. Doctors and nurses walking up and down the aisles, checking on the wounded. He suddenly remembered his friends. He saw a stretcher with a sheet pulled up to cover an entire body. *Chrissy! Is it her?* Cam stumbled and fell against his brother, pulling them both to the floor.

It's probably Ava. It's Ava under the sheet. Dead.

Someone grabbed him under the arms and sat him on a stretcher. "Easy, son. We'll get you checked out soon as we can." Someone else gave him a cup of water, but he couldn't hold it in his hands. It spilled on his lap. "Shorry. Sho…shorry."

"Cammy? Why are you talking funny?"

Cam shrugged and closed his eyes. He heard someone talking about him. "They're the Mitchell boys—Susan and Bill's sons. The young one, Peter, was reported missing. I'll send word that they're both here."

"This little guy seems okay. The older one looks pretty bashed up."

Cam struggled to speak. "Tell...tell I find my brof... Peesher."

"You're silly, Cammy!" Peter was trying to smile, but his eyes were wide with worry.

Cam wanted to hug his little brother, tell him everything would be okay. But he couldn't get his thinking straight. He needed to lie down. Lie down and sleep. Sleep forever.

"We need you to keep sitting up, son. Just until we finish checking you out. You've got a couple of nasty cuts on your head."

Cam nodded, but as soon as the doctor moved along, he slumped over onto his side and closed his eyes.

He could smell Ava's perfume, and her hair tickled his lips. She put her leg over his and whispered, "My man." She leaned in to kiss him. But her face—there was something wrong with her face. It was covered with blood. His heart started to beat wildly. He couldn't breathe.

Cam felt hands lifting him up, carrying him. Peter was crying, calling his name. *Have to save Peter. The ditch. He's drowning. It's my fault. All my fault. Not your fault, Mom. All mine.*

Then a finger tugged at his eyelids. A light shone in his eyes.

Someone yelled, "Need help over here!" Then more hands lifting. His body strapped. Then a whirring noise. A great, loud whirring. Like a blender. Like he was inside a blender.

No! he tried to scream. *No! No! No!* The tornado. He was trapped in the tornado again. He thrashed from side to side. Couldn't move. Someone held his arm. A prick and then…

He was floating. Floating in the air. Calm. *In the eye of the tornado. I made it to the center. No one can hurt me here. Ava! Take my hand. We need to stay together.*

Chapter Eleven

"Concussion...bleeding in the brain...trauma..."

Words floated in and out of Cam's awareness.

As soon as he opened his eyes, Peter jumped on him. "Cam-Cammy! You're awake!"

Their mom gently urged him to get down. "Peter, you need to be careful. You don't want to hurt him."

"Oh now, Susan," said their dad. *Not your dad.* "Seems like nothing can hurt that boy."

Cam tried, but he couldn't keep his eyes open.

Ava? Are you here? I told you to follow me.

I did. I did follow you. But then I couldn't.

"Cam? Can you hear me, Cam? I'm Dr. Gupta. Squeeze my hand if you can hear me."

Cam squeezed as hard as he could.

"Excellent. Can you open your eyes?"

Open your eyes, my man. It's not your time.

Will you be with me, Ava?

It's all right, Cam. I'm okay. Go back. Go on. Do it for me.

"Open your eyes, Cammy," begged Peter. "Doctor says so."

For a brief moment Cam just couldn't decide. *Peter? Ava?*

Please, Cam. I'll always love you. Forever.

"I know you can hear me, Cam," said Dr. Gupta. "Please open your eyes."

Okay. But not because you asked. Because of Ava. Because she told me to. And he opened his eyes.

"Oh thank god. Oh thank…" His mom wiped away tears and put her arms around her husband.

Cam looked around. He was in a hospital room. Peter sat cross-legged at the foot of his bed.

Dr. Gupta smiled at Cam. "Good for you," she said. "One of my best patients." She stepped back to talk to his parents.

"They op'rated, Cammy," said Peter. "On your head. 'Cause you had bleeding."

Cam put a hand to his head and felt bandages.

"They said you coulda died, Cammy, and I said no, 'cause you're Super Brother." Then Peter flopped down on Cam's chest.

Cam pushed himself to sitting. He was stiff, and he felt weak, but he wasn't in any pain. "What day is it, Peter?"

"Monday. I know that because Mondays we have chicken fingers!" said Peter. "And the doctor said that tomorrow you can come home. Because you aren't sick anymore."

"That's right, Cam," Dr. Gupta said. "You suffered severe head trauma. That caused bleeding inside the skull and swelling. But the surgery was successful. If all goes well, we will send you home in twenty-four hours."

Home?

"Mr. Khan said we can stay with them for now," his mom said, guessing what Cam was thinking. "Everyone's helping out however they can."

"And me and Sammy gets to have a sleepover every day!" Peter said very loudly.

"That's enough, Peter," said his dad, scooping Peter off Cam's bed. "We have to go now. Lots of work to do." He didn't seem able to look directly at Cam. "Get some rest."

Cam's mom leaned over and kissed him gently. "I'm so sorry," she whispered. "Things are going to be better. I'm going to be better. I promise." Then she walked out of the room, hurrying to catch up to the doctor.

At the door, his dad turned back. "Take it easy," he said. "I'm sorry about—about all of this. We'll..." He coughed. Then he stared at Cam for a moment before continuing. "We'll talk later. Okay?" He didn't wait for an answer.

Cam fell back on his pillow and slept.

As the day went on, nurses came in and checked on him. One of them took out the intravenous lines in his arm. Someone else had him sit up and eat "real" food. After he'd taken another nap, a physical therapist got him on his feet and asked him to walk.

He shuffled down the hall, limping.

"They had to put a few stitches in that foot," the therapist told him. "And a few more in a whole bunch of other places as well." He shook his head. "Man, you really took a beating, huh?"

Cam nodded. "Yeah, on the highway on Friday. Got sucked out of the car. Into the—" He smiled. He had almost said *tomato*. "Tornado."

"So crazy that happened, right?" said the therapist. "There's a girl down the hall about your age. She has a similar story."

Cam stopped walking and grabbed for the handrail on the hospital wall.

"Whoa! Are you okay?"

Cam nodded. "The girl. What room is she in?" His heart pounded.

"I'll take you there. She won't be walking for some time, but I'm sure she'd love the company," the therapist said.

And before Cam could refuse, he was at the door of room 412.

"Hey, Chrissy, I brought you a visitor. He was caught in the tornado too."

For a moment, Cam and Chrissy just stared at each other. *She hates me! She—*

Then Chrissy gasped and smiled. "Cam! Oh my god! Cam! Mom said you were okay and—" She stopped talking. "But you're not okay, are you?"

"I'll leave you two alone," the therapist said.

Cam sat on the edge of the bed. Chrissy's legs were in traction, raised a couple of feet in the air. "Yeah, both my legs are broken," said Chrissy. "Several places. What about you?"

"Brain injury. A few other things. Some stitches."

Chrissy began to cry. "What happened, Cam? Do you remember? I know Ava and...Adam..." She sobbed and turned her head into the pillow. "I know they're dead."

So Cam told her. About seeing the car. Knowing there was nothing he could do to help. Then he took a deep breath and lied.

"I thought you were dead too. I didn't know..." And he waited to see her reaction.

"Well, of course you did. And what could you have done anyway if you thought I was alive?"

Well, I could have stayed with you until help came. I left you to die alone.

"My parents said an emergency team found me really soon. They said I was lucky I wasn't in the car. I must have fallen out before it smashed into the rock."

Cam looked down. *Change the subject!* "How long will you be in here?"

"I don't know. I'll need lots of rehab and—" Chrissy stopped and looked at Cam.

"And?"

"Cam, I have these awful dreams. I keep seeing the tornado coming. And I wake up screaming. I keep seeing...Ava and Adam, their bodies. I saw them in the car when they carried me to the ambulance." She shuddered.

"I know! Ava's face was—" Cam broke down and started to cry softly.

Chrissy reached for his hand and squeezed. "It's okay, Cam. You're okay. Hey, you want to know something strange? I also have this dream that you talked to me."

Cam kept holding Chrissy's hand, but he couldn't look at her. "Um. I'm getting out of here tomorrow, so I don't know when I'll see you again."

"Will you be going to the funeral?" asked Chrissy. "I heard they decided to do a double one." She let go of Cam's hand and gestured toward her legs. "Obviously, I can't go."

Cam looked out the window. "I'm not sure. I don't think...I don't think they'll want me there."

"What do you mean? Adam was your best friend! And Ava's parents know how much she loved you."

And threatened to ground her if she ever saw me again.

But Cam thought about it for a moment. "Yeah, maybe you're right. Okay. I'll see." He stood up and immediately felt dizzy. "I have to lie down."

He made it back to his room on his own. He stood in the bathroom and stared at himself in the mirror. They had shaved his head. One side was wrapped in gauze. He took off the robe and pulled at the hospital gown. Let it drop to the floor. Stood there naked.

His body was a mess. So many bandages. Stitches everywhere. Great patches of yellow disinfectant splashed all over him. His fingers taped together. A bandage wrapped around one foot. Bruises. Scrapes. Swelling.

And my mind? What can they do for that?

There were no drugs to help him sleep that night. Cam lay awake, counting the hours. He kept seeing his friends. The agony on their faces. Reliving his terror.

And wondering what waited for him at "home."

Chapter Twelve

Cam's dad checked him out of the hospital the next morning.

"Where's Mom?" Cam felt very nervous being alone with him.

"AA meeting. Found a women-only group nearby. I told her to go. Get this thing started."

They got in the pickup and drove out of the city. Cam knew he'd been airlifted to City Hospital on

Friday night. Now he and his dad had to drive the highway back up north to Oakwood.

When they passed the burger place in Halton, Cam started shaking. He couldn't breathe.

"Is this near the spot where it happened?"

Cam couldn't speak. His body was clammy. He nodded and pointed.

His dad pulled over and stopped the truck. "Let's get out." He went around to Cam's side and opened the door. "Come on. We'll walk through this together." He put his arm around Cam's shoulders. "Tell me what happened."

Cam shut his eyes. Saw the whole thing happening in slow motion. Finally he began talking. He pointed to the tree. Showed his dad where the car was. Where he had found Adam and Ava. And then told him the truth about Chrissy.

"I knew you'd be mad about Peter. So I left her. Alone. I could have waited five more minutes. Just five minutes! Until the ambulance showed up. But

I thought she was a goner...and I was scared to be with someone who was dying...and I was scared of you, how mad you'd be." He took a deep breath. "I'm a coward."

"Is that what you think?" his dad asked. "That you're a coward?" He looked up at the sky, sighing deeply. "Look. We all do things we're ashamed of. I know I did. Telling you that you're not my son, for one. It's not an excuse, but I was terrified. My house was gone. I didn't know where Peter was. I was mad at my wife, so mad. And I took it out on you. I blamed you for all of it. But it's not true. And I wish more than anything that I could take it all back."

"But it's the truth," said Cam. "You're *not* my dad."

"Now you listen here, son. I've been your dad for over sixteen years. Nothing can change that. *Nothing.*" Cam was surprised to see him choking up. "And when I saw you in the hospital...thought you were dying..."

Cam tried to change the subject before they both started crying. "What about you and Mom?"

"We're working on it," said his dad. "Maybe we'll get some professional help. We both want to rebuild the house. See what the insurance company says. Maybe we can work on rebuilding our family at the same time."

They began walking back to the truck. "Peter told us how you rescued him. And how you protected him from those looters. So don't you ever call yourself a coward again." He turned Cam around to look right at him. "You hear me?"

Cam nodded. The relief he felt was indescribable.

"Good. Sometimes it takes some real bad crap to help you figure out what kind of a man you are." He looked away. "What kind of a father you are."

They drove back into their town along streets cleared of rubble. Bulldozers were everywhere, pushing wreckage out of the way. Dump trucks were filled to the brim. Cam saw a big X on what was left of several houses.

"What's that?"

"Crews marked each house with an X after they had finished searching. Looking for dead or wounded."

"How many...dead?"

"Fifteen in Oakwood. Over a hundred injured. Still haven't found the Singhs' little girl."

They passed the high school. Cam stared at the wreckage. "I forgot all about school. What's going to happen?"

"Seeing how it's the end of June, they're going to average out the marks. No final exams."

"Guess I failed then. I really screwed up this year."

"Listen, Cam, we all have. We'll get through it together."

They turned down their lane. The fallen trees had been pulled out of the way. The rowboat was gone.

Cam saw his uncle's trailer in the front yard.

"Your aunt and uncle are loading up everything they can find that isn't broken. Keeping it for us until we have a chance to rebuild."

They met up with the rest of the family over at the Khans' place. His aunt and uncle, his mom and Peter were all excited to see him. Everyone asked so many questions. Peter and Sammy wouldn't leave him alone.

After supper Cam's head began pounding. Mrs. Khan noticed before anyone else. "Time for you to rest, Cam. I've got a bed made up for you." She led him downstairs to the basement. "I'll keep the two monsters away. Try to get some sleep."

Cam closed the door and fell on the bed. Didn't bother to get undressed. He tried not to think about what he had to face the next day.

Chapter Thirteen

The funeral service was over. The undertakers had wheeled the two caskets outside. Everyone lined up to pay their final respects. It seemed like the whole town was there. Cam could see Ava's and Adam's parents standing close together. It looked like they were holding each other up.

Cam couldn't delay this any longer. He had to get in line and move forward. He wished he was invisible. But his shaved head, the bandage on the back of his skull, the wounds on his hands and arms—people were definitely staring.

His friend Jake came over and clapped him on the shoulder. "Hey, Cam. That must have been so weird. You have to give us the details, buddy. You doing anything later?"

Moron. "Some other time," Cam said and walked over to the line.

Someone put an arm over his shoulder. "Glad you made it, Cam," said his teacher. "If you ever want to talk…"

"Thanks, Mr. Morgan. Maybe…someday."

The line of people had moved up, and he soon found himself face-to-face with Ava's mother.

Her eyes were dull. No makeup on. She looked old, so much older than she had just a few days ago. Cam wasn't sure if she knew who he was. Ava's dad didn't look so great either.

Adam's parents were just off to the side. Were they

watching him? It seemed to Cam that resentment and anger poured out from every cell of their bodies.

Just do it. Get it over with.

Cam looked down at the ground. "I'm sorry," he mumbled. "Real sorry." He hoped that was enough and started to move away. But then two thoughts came into his mind.

He remembered his dad telling him that sometimes it takes some real bad crap to help you figure out what kind of man you were. And Ava calling Cam "her man."

And so he lifted his head up and looked at all of them. "Adam was my best friend," he managed to say. "And I loved Ava. I miss them both so much." He held back a sob before getting out the rest of his words. "I am so sorry for your loss."

No one answered him. Cam dropped his head.

"Cam." Ava's dad touched his arm. "Thank you." He cleared his throat. "You take care."

Cam nodded and moved along. Shaking hands,

mumbling "sorry" to family members he'd never met but who he knew must be feeling as wrecked as he did. When he got to the last person, he felt lost. He didn't want to listen to the speeches and eat sandwiches at the reception. He couldn't look at the photos of him and his friends from a different time. He spotted his parents watching him and walked toward them.

"Are you okay, honey?" his mom asked. "We don't have to stay." Cam sagged with relief. "Why don't we get you home?"

They got in the car and Cam slumped in the back seat. He looked out the window as they drove past the marina. All the boats had been destroyed.

So no perfect summer job.

His dad was saying something. "The cement anchors were pulled up from the bottom of the lake. Boats tossed about like popcorn."

That's how I feel. Nothing to hold me in place. No anchor.

A row of army vehicles passed them going the other direction.

"They were great," his dad said. "The army. Couldn't have managed without them."

Cam remembered the young cadet. How he had sounded so sure of himself. How he had helped Cam and Peter in the store. Riding with them and making sure they got medical attention in the barracks.

An idea floated into his thoughts. *Crazy.* It was nothing he had ever wanted to do in his old life. But that life was gone.

They pulled into the yard. A bulldozer was knocking down what was left of the house.

"We have to lay down new foundations," his dad explained. "Stronger ones."

Something clicked, and the crazy idea just felt right.

Soon, maybe next week, he'd go over to Bolton. To the barracks. See about joining the Cadets.

New foundations. An anchor. It might sound cheesy, but it was a way forward. And for Cam right now, that was enough.

Acknowledgments

Although this story is fictional, some of the facts are specific to the tornado that swept through Barrie, Ontario, and the surrounding area on May 31, 1985, killing eight people. I am indebted to CBC News coverage of the event. Driving north from Toronto a few weeks later, I saw firsthand the damage done.

Sharon Jennings is the award-winning author of over seventy books for young people, including *The Bye-Bye Pie*, winner of the Blue Spruce Award (Durham), and *Home Free*, which was a finalist for the Governor General's Literary Award and the TD Canadian Children's Literature Award. Sharon teaches writing, works as a freelance editor and manuscript reviewer, and gives workshops and speeches across the country. She is also the president of CANSCAIP. She lives in Toronto.